# The G
# Feather Gang

## Antony Wootten

Toby! I hope you enjoy this story. Best wishes! AWootten

Eskdale Publishing
www.antonywootten.co.uk

Eskdale Publishing, UK

First published in Great Britain in 2015 by Eskdale Publishing, North Yorkshire

**www.antonywootten.co.uk**

A Catalogue record for this book is available from the British Library.

ISBN: 978-0-9537123-8-0

**Printed and bound in the UK by**

**York Publishing Services**
**www.yps-publishing.co.uk**

# The Grubby Feather Gang

# Upside-down

George decided the world looked slightly better upside-down. The trees on the ridge seemed to be dangling into the blue sky, and the horses looked as if they were standing on the green ceiling of the world like the spiders on the wooden beams in his kitchen. Maybe, if the world really did turn upside-down, all the bad things would fall off it and all the good things would somehow, magically, stay put.

He could feel the weight of his own blood in his head and face, and his arms hung heavily beneath him. Strangely, he didn't really mind. Not many people got to see the world like this. It was almost worth being bullied.

"Are you ready to give in yet," said Stan, "or should I let you fall?"

George was beginning to lose track of how long he had been hanging there, upside-down, from the opening high in the outside wall of the barn. Like a trapeze artist, his legs were bent over the opening's jagged wooden edge onto the floorboards of the hayloft, where Stan was holding him there by sitting

1

on his ankles.

There was a long drop beneath him to the stony ground, but if he fell, perhaps that would be an end to it: no more being bullied by Stan; no more feeling sick that everyone in the village hated him; no more worrying about his dad and mum fighting all the time, about the women calling his dad a coward because he hadn't gone to fight in the war, about the children at school keeping away from him as if he smelt.

"Let me fall, I don't care," George said. "If I die, you'll go to prison."

"You wouldn't die," Stan protested, as if he'd thought this through carefully.

"I bloomin' well might. It's a heck of a long way down."

"No it's not," Stan said, sounding hurt, as if he hadn't meant to put George in danger. That was the strange thing about Stan: he acted like the bully, but sometimes he talked like the victim.

"It is," George said, calmly. "If I fall now, I'll burst open like an egg, and you'll go to prison." George couldn't help himself. He always knew how to get Stan riled, and he couldn't resist, even now. "They'll probably hang you."

2

"Right, that's it, I'm going to drop you unless you give in right now, you runt," Stan said crossly. "I can't hold you anymore, you're too fat."

"Can't be a runt *and* fat," George informed him.

"*You* can," Stan snapped back, and he slackened his grip. George felt his heart lurch as his legs came free, and he realised he wasn't ready to die yet. Stan wasn't ready to let him either, and, after a brief shriek of panic, George felt Stan's full weight slamming his calves back down onto the floorboards. "Hah!" Stan laughed. "You screamed like a girl! No wonder your dad's a coward."

George decided not to comment on the fact that that didn't make sense. He wouldn't be drawn into a conversation about his father. Those always got him confused and angry, and made him feel like crying. So instead he said, "Wait, Stan, I think I can see your mum coming over the hill."

"Where?" Stan said, sounding a little worried.

"Oh hang on, my mistake," George went on. "It's only a cow." He'd never even seen Stan's mum and he felt a bit guilty about insulting her, but not for long.

"Right, that's it," Stan said again. George felt Stan shifting himself so that he was sitting on

George's shins, holding him in place with his body weight. Then George saw him leaning out over the top of him, his silly face looming there like an approaching zeppelin.

"Ugh, you could have warned me I was going to have to look at you," George said. "I've just eaten."

"Eat this," Stan said, and for a moment George wondered what he was doing. But when he saw the foamy glob appearing at Stan's lips he quickly realised.

"That's disgusting!" George squawked, pressing himself against the barn wall in a desperate attempt to avoid the foul ball of spit which Stan was about to let drop. "Ugh, you're disgusting!" George said as the globule hung over him on an ever-weakening strand of saliva. "I don't want your germs! I don't want your lurgy! I don't want to catch stupid-disease!" George was shielding his face with his arms, and the bloated spit ball broke free, landing on his elbow and splashing itself across his cheek. He wiped it away wildly. Stan let out a loud, triumphant laugh. "Eargh!" George yelled. "Help! It burns! It burns!" It didn't burn, but it was foul. "The spit of a moron! It's infecting me! I can feel my brain melting! I'm turning stupid already!"

# Chapter 1: Upside-down

"Shut up," Stan said. "Shut up, runt, or I'll do it again." And he began the preparations by noisily hawking something horrible into his mouth.

"Alright, alright!" George cried, defeated. "I'll do your stupid homework."

"Well, why didn't you just say that in the first place?" Stan said, forming the words awkwardly round the bolus of gob he was keeping in his mouth as a precautionary measure. He swallowed it and said, "Come on, I'll help you up."

A minute or two later, George was sitting on the boards of the barn's hayloft, rubbing the backs of his legs, and allowing the blood to redistribute itself around his body now that he was the right way up again. Stan pulled his maths book from his satchel. "Here y'are," he said, handing it to George. Reluctantly, George took it and slid it into his own satchel. In all honesty, he actually quite liked long-multiplication.

"Okay," Stan said, sounding all friendly now. As he climbed down the ladder from the hayloft, he said, "Give it to me at the gate tomorrow. See ya!" and off he ran leaving George sitting there in the gloom, alone.

Or at least, he thought he was alone until he

5

heard a little voice saying, "You ain't gonna let him get away with that, are you?"

George almost jumped out of his skin. "Who's there?" he said timidly.

There was a rustle from the mound of hay which took up much of the space up here in the hayloft, and the small, ragged figure of a girl emerged from within it. She took a few moments to brush away the hay, pulling some from her wild, curly hair and smoothing her tatty dress. "I saw the whole thing," she said.

"You saw... Why didn't you do something?"

"Why didn't *you* do something?" she snapped straight back at him. "Are you a coward?"

George thought about that. Then he said, "Yes, I think so."

"What?" the girl said, horrified. "Well, don't be!"

"Don't be a coward?"

"Yes!"

"But... I can't make myself suddenly be really strong and fight him. He's stronger than me. I'm fat and short. I can't help that."

"Actually," the girl said, her tone softening, "you ain't a coward. If you was a coward, you wouldn't of spoken to him like that. You wouldn't of called his mum a cow, and told him he was stupid, would ya?"

"I dunno," George said, thinking about that for a moment. "But still, you could have done something. Why didn't you help me? You could have gone and got someone."

"I ain't here to fight your battles for you. I wanted to see what you'd do."

"Oh." George said. "What if he'd dropped me? What if I'd fallen to my death?"

"Well, I'd have thanked my lucky stars for the ringside seat!"

"Oh, that's kind," George said, sarcastically. He looked at the girl. She was about his age, grubby and feral looking, with straw sticking out of her hair and an old dress that was full of holes. She had a chirpy expression though, almost pretty. There was something about her that made him feel like grinning. "What's your name?" he said.

"Emma. What's yours?"

"George."

From down below in the barn there came a loud, plaintive meow. "Oh, Azar," Emma cried in apparent irritation, and leaned over the edge of the hayloft. "What you doing here? Leave me alone won't

7

you?" To George, she explained, "Bloomin' cat follows me everywhere. I hate cats!"

"I love them, but they make me sneeze," George said. "My dad's a vet, so I get to see lots of cats, but I start sneezing if I stroke them. Come on," and he climbed down the ladder, his satchel slung across his body.

The cat, a scrawny white thing that looked as if it had never learned to clean itself, meowed at him, and he meowed back. He wanted to stroke it but knew his eyes would puff up and water, and his throat would itch, and he'd have a sneezing fit. Emma arrived beside him. "Go home, Azar," she said crossly, and waved the cat away, but it ignored her completely and curled itself affectionately around her leg. "Azar!" she scolded, but crouched down and scratched it softly behind the ears anyway. "Go home," she snapped. "Stop following me you mangy fleabag," she said as she stroked its long back.

"Where do you live?" George said, wondering why he'd never seen her before.

"Here. This is my uncle's farm. I was hiding in the hay from my aunt. She gets me doing chores."

"Why have I never seen you at school?"

"I've only been here for a few days. Going to

start school tomorrow." They were outside now. There was a cool spring breeze, and the budding trees seemed to glow in the light of the afternoon sun.

"Oh, I'll see you there then," George said, unsure of how he felt about his strange new classmate.

"Probably," Emma said, and off she ran, along the rutted lane, the white cat skipping and bouncing along behind her.

# George's Plan

As usual, George's mother seemed in a good spirits until his father arrived home from his rounds. He came in smiling, and his cheerfulness filled the room, but George's mother barely spoke to him. They all had their dinner in virtual silence, although his father winked at George every now and then to tell him it would all be alright, but George wondered if his mother would ever stop being cross. Dad wasn't the only man in the village to refuse to go away and fight. It wasn't his fault men were dying in France.

After dinner, George had to fetch wood for the range, take out the ashes and sweep the kitchen floor, but he got on with these and his other chores without complaint. He didn't want to anger his mother tonight. Then, he slipped away upstairs to his tiny room. He opened the window to let in some cool air. The sun was dipping now, but he didn't need to light a candle yet. He sat on his bed and pulled the books from his satchel. He laid his and Stan's books out beside him. First, as dusk descended on the village, he worked his way through the twenty long-multiplication sums in his own book. He packed that away in his satchel, and opened Stan's book. He had a plan which would ensure Stan would never make him do his homework again. He'd done homework for Stan before, and had always done it correctly, but that tradition would end tonight. Sum after sum he completed neatly and tidily, but with completely the wrong answer. Smiling to himself, engrossed in his happy fantasy of the punishment that would be inflicted on Stan for his hopelessness, he didn't notice his mother's footsteps on the stairs, and he jumped when the door opened.

"Hello my love," his mum said, coming into the room.

"Hi Mum."

"Homework?"

"Yep."

"Let me see. I like to know how you're doing." George froze. He really didn't want her to see him doing someone else's homework. She wouldn't like that. But there was nothing he could do. He watched as his mum picked up Stan's book. Maybe she wouldn't notice. George held his breath as she perched on the bed beside him, her long dress rustling, and he could see her mind working as she silently checked the sums.

"Um..." she began after a moment. She lowered the book and looked at George, then raised it again and checked a few more, then dropped it into her lap. "These are... These are all wrong, my love," she said softly, danger lurking beneath her gentle tone. "Are you just not trying? I know you can do these." George said nothing. His mum picked up the book again and began leafing through the pages. She gazed down on page after page of the sums Stan had done in class. Stan's work was messy and full of mistakes which Mr Haxby, the schoolmaster, had corrected. She hardly seemed to be breathing now, and George noticed the room had become cold and dark.

Suddenly, as if struck by a realisation, George's mum glanced at the cover of the book. Stan's name must have leapt out at her. She turned her face towards George, an unreadable expression on her lips. "George, my love," she breathed, "tell me why you are doing Stan's homework."

"Um..."

"George," she said with a note of warning.

"He held me upside down from the hayloft, Mum!" George blurted.

"What?"

"Don't say anything, Mum. Don't tell Mr

12

Haxby."

"Why would I do that?" she said, darkly. George felt himself shrivel under the weight of her judgement.

"I don't know..."

Very slowly, she put the books down, stood, and went over to the window. She leaned against the sill, her back to him, and the deepening twilight glowed around her. Without turning, she said, "George, there are bad people in this world, and if you let them walk all over you once, they will do it again and again. You do know that, don't you?"

George nodded. "I have got the sums all wrong, to get him into trouble," he contested. But his mother looked at him with a disappointed expression. It was the same one she used on his father when he contested that he was writing letters to all and sundry to impress upon them the futility of war.

Shame burned in George's chest.

His mother stood facing him now, silhouetted against the dusk. "This is what you are to do." She came towards him, and towered over him like a thundercloud. "You are to punch him. Do you hear me?" She wasn't raising her voice, but she was driving her words into him with frightening force.

"Punch him. I don't care where or how, but you punch him hard. Do you hear me?" George nodded. "What are you going to do?"

George could hardly bring himself to speak.

"What are you going to do?"

"Punch him."

"Good." His mother bent forwards then, cupped his face in her hands and kissed his head. "Good boy," she said. "You have to fight bullies, George. That's something your father doesn't seem to understand." And with that, she went, leaving George feeling sick and ashamed. He'd never punched anyone in his life. He wasn't even sure he knew how. Anger sizzled inside him. He'd never had a fight with Stan, but he was pretty sure he knew what would happen if he did. Stan would win easily, just like he'd easily pushed George out of the hayloft doorway and hung him upside down. George hadn't even tried to stop him. He didn't know how.

# The Feather

The next morning, George rose with a sense of anxious excitement. He knew that what he'd planned was cruel, but, as his mother had said, you have to stand up to bullies. Okay, so he wasn't going to punch Stan, but his plan would certainly teach Stan a lesson. Before breakfast, George had to run out to the milk cart to collect a small bucket of milk which he struggled to carry. Just as he was pushing the garden gate shut with his foot, a girl ran across the street towards him.

"Is your dad there?" she said. She didn't look happy. George recognised her. She was older than him by a few years, and lived just across the other side of the village green. George, guessing what was coming, lied, saying that he'd already left for a meeting somewhere.

"Oh," the girl said. Her eyes looked red, as if she'd been crying. Then, she held out a white feather. George looked at it. He knew what it meant, but he didn't take it. "It's a feather," the girl said, "for your dad."

Just then George's father came out of the house.

"Oh, hello Maggie," he said warmly. "I thought that was you. I've heard the awful news about your brother. I'm ever so sorry."

"Coward," Maggie spat with sudden ferocious hatred. "Here, take this," and she handed him the feather.

"Thank you, my dear," George's father said, taking it from her as if it was a welcome gift.

"Men like you make me sick," Maggie went on. "My brother..." she seemed briefly to choke, and a tear broke from one eye. "My brother..." she went on bravely, "he fought... he fought to protect his country, and all you do is sit around letting others do the fighting and dying. You should be ashamed."

"Maggie," George's father said, his tone filled with sympathy for the poor girl. "I am not ashamed, but I do understand and respect your feelings. There is more than one way to fight, though."

George turned to go back inside, but his father seemed to be deliberately blocking his way, as if he *wanted* George to see the humiliating exchange.

"And what way do you fight? By writing letters to the prime minister? How are you helping our boys? I bet you think my brother deserved to be killed. I bet you think they all do."

"I certainly do not think that, Maggie," George's father said, firmly, but without even a hint of anger in his voice. "I wholeheartedly believe that all men who go to war are brave and courageous —"

"But wicked? That's what you think, isn't it? It's wicked to fight."

"No. It is not wicked to fight to defend your country. Your brother was a good man."

"Then why aren't you out there fighting?"

"Because I believe that war is wrong." A couple of other women who had been heading for the milk cart had gravitated towards the conversation now. George wished he could disappear into the soil, like rain. He could not believe his dad would stand there and let these women hate him and hurl abuse at him. But his father always took the abuse calmly and almost... *gratefully*.

One of the other women, angered by what she had heard, chimed in, "You believe war is wrong? So our boys and men are doing wrong are they? That is an insult to their bravery."

"I believe war is wrong, but I do believe our boys and men are good people. They are brave and good. I love and respect them for what they are doing. But, but... war is wrong, and I refuse to join in.

Instead, I will —"

"Coward!" someone shouted.

"Coward!" Maggie echoed. "You're a filthy coward."

"Instead, I will..." George's father went on, undeterred, "I will fight *war itself*. Next week, I will —"

"You make me sick," someone else shouted. Quite a crowd of women and children had gathered now, and beyond them, the old man driving the milk cart, also watched. He was too old to be a soldier, but not too old to give George's father a foul glare of hatred. "You should be put in prison for desertion," one of the women said. George felt the hot prickle of tears building in his eyes and he was determined not to let anyone see him cry. Why did his father always try to talk to these people?

"For treason!" someone else added.

"Should be shot!" came another voice, filled with spite.

"Next week," George's father calmly went on, "I will be travelling to London to lobby Parliament to find a peaceful way to end the war. There are many very clever people with very strong ideas about how we could achieve peace and end the fighting —"

"Utter rubbish!" a woman called. "Parliament aren't going to listen to you, you jumped-up fool! What makes you think you're so important?"

"It is not just me, my dear. I am indeed a man of very little importance, but there are important, powerful men – and women, I should add – who feel exactly the same as me, and who will also be lobbying —"

The crowd interrupted as one, a cacophony of jeers and noise. Someone threw a clod of soil which hit George's father's arm, some of it splashing into the milk. Through the film of tears which George refused to let fall, he saw the white feather held delicately in his father's fingers. His father always kept the feathers he was presented with. They were a symbol of cowardice, but he kept them, and displayed them on the mantelpiece as if they were trophies. George could not understand why. He turned away from the angry women, and blinked heavily, finally letting the tears drop to the ground. He screwed his eyes up as if they were sponges he was wringing out, to make sure all the tears had gone, and then he saw his mother coming out of the cottage.

"Go home, all of you," she said in her level, yet fearsome, tone. But her power had little effect on the crowd.

"Have a word with yer man, Liz," one of the women instructed her. "He's a good-for-nothing." And the shouting began again.

George's mother didn't reply to that. His father nodded, thanked Maggie for the feather, and, turning away from the baying crowd, the three of them headed inside.

George heaved the heavy bucket of spoilt milk up onto the table, and his father began the ritual of nailing the fresh feather onto the long piece of wood on the mantelpiece which was already adorned with many others. George's mother stood there with her clenched fists on her hips, watching him. George felt the crushing weight of dread building in the room, and his father stepped back to admire his handiwork.

"I suppose you're happy now," George's mother said. "Got another one to add to your collection."

"Soon I'll have a whole chicken," George's father joked, as always. His mother was not amused. His father turned. He took a step towards her, reached forwards and took her hands gently in his. To George's relief, she allowed him to uncurl her fingers and kiss them. George felt the dread easing off, as if a window had been opened letting the bad feelings escape into the morning air. "My love," George's father said. "Those feathers... They certainly do not make me happy. But, as I've told you before, they make me *question* myself. Every time I see that row of white feathers, I am forced to ask myself, 'am I doing the right thing?'"

"And you continue to believe you are?"

"Indeed I do, dear wife."

At this, his mother snatched her hands away. Dread surged back into the room as she glared at him and shook her head. She needed no words, her feelings were palpable, and George's father looked defeated as he watched her storm out, slamming the back door so hard the cottage shook.

"George," his father said, slowly lowering himself into the rocking chair beside the fire. "I know how hard this must be for you. Those people out there, they are right. They *really are right*," he said, and he laughed a little. "But so am I. I don't know what you think of me. Do you think I'm a coward, my son?" George did not know what to say. He thought the answer was probably 'yes', but he loved his father even so, and was glad he hadn't gone to fight in the war. So, he shook his head. "Hmmm," his father said. "I'm not so sure I believe you. And it breaks my heart to imagine you might think that of me, and worse, that you might be right to think it. But... I still have to do what I believe is right. I will not fight in the war. But I will fight *war itself*, in whatever way I can."

# The Cane

When George left for school a little later, some of the women were still standing around nearby, in small, chattering groups. Keeping his head down, he hurried past them.

"Hey," someone called. It was Maggie, the one who had brought today's feather. "I didn't mean any harm to you," she called after him. He stopped, and wondered if he should say something to that. He didn't know what to think of these people. Even his father had said they were right. Should he hate them? Fear them? Be angry with them? He didn't feel any of those things, just an emptiness. After a moment, he hurried on without even looking at her.

Several minutes later he reached the school which was a long, stone building with arched windows all along one side, a bit like a church. He was about to head inside when Stan came lolloping up to him like a happy puppy. "George!" he barked playfully. Sometimes it seemed Stan had no recollection of his own actions and thought they were the best of friends. "Alright?" He was panting from running.

"Yep," George said.

"Give us me book," Stan said expectantly. George dug it out of his satchel and handed it to him. Stan could be good fun, and when he was in a friendly mood like this George didn't mind his company. He'd completely forgotten about getting all the sums wrong, and, remembering suddenly, he hesitated to let go of the book. "Oi!" Stan objected, oblivious. "Let go!" George did, and felt a stab of guilt. He could really do with a friend today.

"Go away, cat!" came a newly familiar voice behind him. Turning, he saw Emma shooing her scrawny, white follower away. "Go away! I don't like you!" she squawked at it, flapping her hands at it and then stroking its ears.

Once inside, George nodded in greeting to Emma. Mr Haxby showed Emma to her desk and quietly laid down a few classroom rules for her. Mr Haxby was a small, mostly bald man with glasses and a thick moustache. He always insisted on wearing his black gown over his suit and tie, even when the room was hot, and consequently he frequently smelt awful. Returning to his lectern at the front of the room, he called the register, closed it and put it away in his desk drawer. Then, he sent a couple of the younger ones around to collect in all the homework books. Emma caught George's eye, and he smiled back. Now that she was there, the brief flash of guilt he'd felt earlier had vanished.

The morning's lessons were long and laborious. George had heard of teachers in other schools taking children out into the fields to study plants and insects on warm spring days like this, but Mr Haxby would never do any such thing. He was a small man who spoke a little too quietly, but you always knew it would be your fault, not his, if you failed to hear an instruction, and he would quickly become unnecessarily angry. All morning, as the children wrote in silence, Mr Haxby worked his way through the stack of homework books on his desk. George felt a strange mixture of excitement and anxiety building in him as he watched the stack diminish: when would his treachery be discovered?

And then it happened.

Looking slowly up from his marking, Mr Haxby said, "North," which was Stan's surname, "come here." Stan stood awkwardly and looked at George. George looked back at him and smiled. Innocently, Stan returned the smile, and, bemused, made his way Mr Haxby's desk.

"Yes, Sir?" he said politely.

Mr Haxby held the book open before Stan's face, making him step back a little in alarm. "Explain," Mr Haxby commanded. Everyone was watching now, Emma included, and George felt a burn of angry pleasure in his throat.

"Um..." Stan began.

"They are all wrong," Mr Haxby snapped.

"That's impossible, Sir," Stan said in disbelief.

"Impossible? Why would you say that?" Mr Haxby said.

"Because..." Stan began, and George quickly pretended to be getting on with his work.

"Why are they all wrong, boy? Do I not teach you well?"

"Oh, yes Sir, you do, but..." Stan had gone red and was looking round at the class now. He really didn't seem to understand what had happened. He just looked completely confused.

"Then what is it?" Mr Haxby said, rising from his seat like a snake uncoiling. "Couldn't be bothered, eh? Wanted to get out and play in the sun, did we? Mmm?"

"No, I..."

"Master North, you do not find mathematics

26

easy at the best of times, and a lesser man than I might have given up on you by now. But I have persevered with you. I know that even you could get some of these right. So what the devil am I to think? Mm?"

Stan looked around, helpless and utterly perplexed. He could not understand why the sums were all wrong. Then, his questioning eyes fell on George. George just shrugged, and smiled.

"Come on, North," Mr Haxby went on. "We both know you can do better than this. Explain."

In a panic, Stan blurted, "It was George!"

"I beg your pardon?" Mr Haxby said, and turned to George. "Do you know anything about this?"

George shook his head.

"He did them for me!" Stan blathered, foolishly.

"I don't know what he's talking about, Sir," George said innocently.

But Mr Haxby was not a fool. He took a moment to study the book, and then rummaged through the other books until he found what he was looking for. George didn't understand at first, but then he was struck by a sudden realisation, and he felt as if his stomach had fallen into a pit. Mr Haxby was looking at George's book. He was comparing the handwriting. George cursed himself for his stupidity. He knew Stan's numbers were always scruffy and often back to front. He hadn't thought about that when he did the sums last night.

"By God," Mr Haxby steamed. "You're right! Sanders," which was George's surname, "get your sorry self here right this instant."

*

"I hate Mr Haxby," George muttered to himself, his hand still stinging horribly from the three strikes of the cane. His eyes were hot and wet, and he watched a tear drop into the dry soil where he sat. It was lunchtime, and he was sitting alone, beneath the tree in the school yard.

"I don't mind him," said a voice, catching him by surprise. With the back of his hand he wiped his eyes hurriedly and looked up. It was Emma.

"You *like* him?" George said, incredulous.

"I said I *don't mind* him," Emma corrected him. "He made my morning very entertaining with all the canings, anyway."

"But he caned me for no reason! It wasn't me who did something wrong, it was Stan!"

"He got caned too," Emma pointed out.

"Yes, but what did *I* get caned for?"

"You shouldn't of done Stan's homework." That was certainly the way Mr Haxby had seen it. Mr Haxby had assumed George had been doing Stan a favour, and George, feeling that people would think he was a coward if he admitted that Stan had actually *made* him do it, had kept his mouth shut and accepted his punishment. But he was furious about it now.

"Hey, George," came a more unwelcome voice.

"What do you want?" George said, getting to his feet as Stan came bouldering over to them.

"What a morning, eh?" Stan said, breathless. To George's surprise, he didn't seem at all cross. "How's your hand? Mine's killing me." He opened it to show George the welt across his palm.

"Good," George snapped, and glared at him. "I hope it *actually kills* you."

Stan looked confused by the reaction. But that wasn't all that confused him. "Why did you get all my sums wrong?" he asked.

"Oh, you finally worked it out then did you?" said George.

Stan said nothing. He actually looked hurt, as if George had really upset him.

29

Antagonistically, George said, "If I'd got any of them right, Haxby would definitely have known you didn't do them."

"Shut up. I'm not as stupid as I look," said Stan.

George just laughed at him, and glanced at Emma, who didn't seem to paying either of them any attention and was instead watching a spider crawl up her arm.

"No, you're *even more* stupid than you look," George said.

"I thought you were my friend," Stan said, eyes wide.

George thought about what his mother had told him to do. Stan wasn't getting the message. He thought it was all a game, all the bullying. He really didn't seem to think he'd done anything wrong. He certainly didn't realise how angry George was. But George was angry, and that anger now surged through his body like steam in a boiler, and exploded out of him in the form of a disappointingly feeble shove to Stan's chest. Stan just looked at George with the mournful expression of a puppy who can't understand why his master has just kicked him. And then he returned the shove. But Stan was taller and stronger, and his shove thrust George backwards against the tree. George cried out in pain and rubbed his head furiously.

"What you going to do?" Stan said. "Go running home to Mummy? Or to Daddy? Do you call him Daddy? Or do you call him Mummy too? Coz he's not really a man, is he? Your daddy's a woman. You've not got a daddy. You've got two mummies."

In George's mind, he punched Stan right on his nose, really hard, just like his mother had told him to. But it was only in his mind. Really, he was afraid Stan would punch *him*, and afraid Emma would see that he was almost crying.

"It's not my fault you're thick," George shouted, his usual wit failing him.

"It's not my fault you're fat," Stan said, and walked away.

George screwed his eyes up, partly in anger and partly to keep the tears inside. It seemed like ages before he could open them again. When he did, he looked around, and saw that Emma was gone.

# Revenge

Satchel across his body, George trudged along, glad that school was over for the day but not wanting to go home. So, instead of sticking to the main road, he meandered through the lanes and fields, until he saw the barn. He hadn't meant to end up there, his feet had just led him there, by accident.

It had begun to rain, so he was glad of the shelter. There was no danger of Stan being here today as Mr Haxby had kept him behind to do his sums. Apart from the stinging palm, George felt he'd probably got off quite lightly himself. He didn't bother climbing to the hayloft. There were several old, disintegrating bales down here, amongst rusting ploughs and abandoned carts. He hoisted himself into the back of one of the carts, and lay on the wooden boards, looking up blankly at the underside of the hayloft.

"Meow!" The sound of a cat startled him.

"Oh, you stupid creature," came Emma's voice. "I was sneaking up on 'im! You've messed it up for me. Stupid cat." George sat up and saw her coming towards him, faithful Azar at her heels. "I was sneaking up on you," she explained.

"I know."

Emma slumped into a loosely tied bale of hay which partly engulfed her.

"You got properly done," she said.

"I know that too."

"Your hand must hurt."

"Nope," George lied.

Emma just laughed at that. "And your head," she added. George didn't reply. "So," Emma went on, "what you gonna do about it then?"

"About what?"

"'About what?'" Emma repeated in consternation. "About Stan, of course!"

"And Mr Haxby," George said.

"Why Mr Haxby?"

"Well, he caned me didn't he? He's always caning people for nothing. I mean... I didn't deserve it. It's not fair."

"Well, he thought you did deserve your caning today," Emma stated. "Alright then, what you gonna do about Stan *and* Mr Haxby then?"

"Well... My mum said I should punch Stan."

"Yeah, you should. I agree with that. But... I don't think you will though, will you? You're not like that."

"Mmm," George muttered, distantly. "I'm a coward."

"Well," Emma said, "I thought you weren't a coward yesterday, but today, all them tears, and not hitting Stan back when he shoved you against the tree..."

"I *wasn't* crying, and I shoved him first," George said defensively.

"Whatever you say. Hey," she said, suddenly remembering something, "What was Stan on about when he said them things about your dad?"

"Nothing," George snapped back quickly.

"Alright, alright, I was only asking." There was a long silence then. After a while, Emma said, "So, your dad's a conchie is he?"

"No," George said sharply. Conchie was short for conscientious objector, someone who refused to fight in the war. It was not a kind term, but it was not as bad as 'coward'. "Yes," he relented, "But he prefers the word 'pacifist'."

"He would," Emma said, chewing thoughtfully on a piece of hay. "Well, I wish everyone was a conchie – alright, pacifist – coz then there'd be no war." That surprised George. He shuffled to the front

34

of the cart and looked down at where she sat. The cat was curled in her lap now, purring. She stopped stroking him when she saw George looking.

"Is your dad a pacifist too?" George asked hopefully.

"Get away," Emma said as if the idea was ridiculous. "He's a proper soldier, fighting in France to save England!"

"Oh," George said, deflated, and lay back down.

"That's why I've had to come here," Emma said. "Ain't got a mum; well, she died when I was little. Dad was looking after me, but he's gone to the war so I've come here."

"Sorry about your mum," George said, feeling as if he ought to.

At first, Emma didn't respond, but after a while she said, "Never liked her anyway." Then, not giving George chance to reply, she said, "Did you know Mr Haxby's a coward?"

"Is he?"

"Well, my uncle said he is. That's what he told me the other day. He doesn't like teachers, my uncle, not men teachers anyway, and he especially doesn't like Mr Haxby. He said Mr Haxby should be away fighting but he's too scared. He's not even a conchie.

35

He said Mr Haxby pretends he has to be here to do the teaching, but he doesn't. He doesn't even *like* teaching! He's soldiering age, and there are lots of women around who could teach us instead of him. He just doesn't want to go and fight." George thought that seemed about right. He knew his dad was trying to do something important at least, and wasn't just shirking his responsibilities because he was scared, but Mr Haxby...

"I thought you said you liked Mr Haxby," George said.

"You know what?" Emma went on, ignoring George's comment, "If you're not going to actually punch either of them, I know how you could get revenge on Stan *and* Mr Haxby, both at the same time!"

"Revenge?" He sat up again, and hung his feet over the open end of the cart.

"Yep! You do want that, don't you?"

Something about Emma's strange, toothy grin, framed in dimples and freckles and wild, ginger ringlets made George feel cheerful. He liked her, and she must like him too, otherwise she wouldn't be talking to him.

"I'm listening," he said.

36

# Emma's Plan

Emma's plan was brilliant! It wouldn't be easy, and if they were caught they would be in real trouble, but this was George's chance to prove he wasn't a coward. So, after his chores that Sunday morning, George hurried to the barn to meet Emma, as they'd arranged.

"Have you got it?" George said as he arrived at the barn, his heart racing.

Emma just pointed to the small, closed cardboard box on the floor around which the cat was prowling. George picked it up, and felt the creature inside squirm a bit. It emitted a low, warning cluck, but other than that, the hen seemed content to stay put in the darkness of the box.

"Come on," Emma said. A few minutes later, they were picking their way through the meadows and wet undergrowth, keeping clear of the main street. Soon, they arrived at the perimeter of the school field. Checking to make sure there was no-one around, they hurried across the field towards the building. In a short while, they were crouching against the school's back door, like burglars.

"Right," Emma said, rummaging in the satchel she was carrying. Out came a long leather pouch, from which she drew a couple of hooked metal implements. George watched, astonished, as she used the lockpicks, wiggling them around and twisting them this way and that. "Where did you get those?" he asked, but Emma shushed him crossly. A moment later, there was a click. Emma withdrew the picks and looked at George.

"What?" said George.

"Try the door, idiot!"

"Oh." Heart pounding, he tried the handle. To his amazement, it opened.

"Quick!" Emma hissed, and shoved him inside. There was a squawk from within the box, and George, in his haste, stumbled to his knees, barely keeping hold of it. Azar slipped in beside them, but Emma scooped him up and sent him straight back out again, clicking the door shut. George could not believe he was doing this. What had Emma got him into? But a quick glance from her cheeky, funny face was all he needed to urge him onwards.

"How did you know how to pick a lock?" George said as they entered the school hall. He could feel panic rising in his throat, but he refused to let it affect him.

"Never you mind, nosey," Emma said.

When they reached the tall cupboard in the corner of the hall, George put the box on the floor. They had talked about this so many times they didn't need to discuss what to do next. They hurried into the classroom, retrieved a small set of keys from Mr Haxby's desk drawer, and headed back to the hall. Quickly, they unlocked the cupboard.

"Will she be alright?" George asked as Emma removed the lid of the box. Inside, an almost completely white hen raised her head and looked around at her new surroundings.

"You damn great softie!" Emma scolded him.

"Alright," George objected. "But she hasn't done anything. *You* wouldn't want to be locked in the cupboard 'til Monday morning, would you?"

"She'll be fine," Emma said, "won't you Snowy?" Snowy hopped out of the box, gave her wings a little stretch, and clucked. "See?"

George wasn't quite sure what he was supposed to 'see', but decided to give Emma the benefit of the doubt. "Go on then," Emma said.

"Oh yes, I almost forgot." A mixture of elation and terror churning inside him, George took a large handful of straw from the box and hurried to the cloakroom. Under the bench beneath the coat hooks, each child had a pair of plimsolls in a shoe box. Stan's was tatty and old, and his name was emblazoned on it in big letters. Quickly, George stuffed some straw into Stan's plimsoll box and scattered the rest around. Then, he hurried back to the hall where Emma was holding Snowy in both hands so she couldn't flap her wings.

Stan got a large sheet of paper out of the cupboard and wrote 'Mr Haxby is a cowod' on it in crayon, in block capitals, like Stan's writing, deliberately spelling it the way Stan might, and nailed it to the inside of the cupboard door. Then, what was left of the straw he scattered into the bottom of the cupboard.

"Right, you'll have to be quick now," Emma instructed. She positioned herself in front of the cupboard, and George nodded to show he was ready. Emma placed Snowy in the bottom of the cupboard and quickly backed away as George closed the door, the hen safely stowed inside. Finally, they hammered a small tack into place, just to make sure the cupboard would need a good jiggle in order to get it open.

"See you tomorrow morning, Snowy," George said.

The trap was set.

As they made their way back out into the sunshine, disposing of the empty box in some nearby nettles, George felt pride and excitement burning inside him. Emma must think he was so brave! And he couldn't wait until Monday morning assembly. Mr Haxby would go to open the cupboard, as always, to retrieve the bible, but the door would be stuck, so he'd jiggle it. That would wake up Snowy, if she wasn't already awake, and get her flapping around inside. Mr Haxby would yank open the door and the hen would flap out at him, white feathers falling all around him like a blizzard. The significance would be clear: not just a single white feather but a whole hen! And the word 'cowod' on the inside of the cupboard door would be there for all to see! The straw in Stan's shoe box, coupled with the fact that they had also left the crayon, some tacks and nails and the hammer in there too, would all lead Mr Haxby to conclude that the culprit was Stan. The plan was foolproof! All they had to do now was go about their normal business, and watch the sequence of events unfold.

\*

Outside, the sky seemed dark, even though it was approaching midday. The threat of thunder loomed over them, but they laughed as they hurried along the overgrown tracks to the farm. Eventually, they arrived in the barn, and fell onto the hay. They lay there reliving their last hour and revelling in their triumph and relief.

"I can't believe we did it!" George cried. "I just can't! Hey, Emma, thanks for helping me." Emma didn't respond. "Why *did* you help me?"

"Wait," Emma said, her mirth suddenly draining from her. "Where's that cat?"

"The cat? Who cares? I thought you hated it!"

"I do, but... Did you see it when we came out of the school?"

"No..."

"Well, he's normally right here, bothering me."

"So?"

"So, now he ain't. Oh no," Emma said, her expression darkening. "You don't think he got in do you, when we came out? We could have locked him in."

"Oh..." The significance dawned on George. If the cat was in the school, Mr Haxby would see it, and then he'd know... "Oh," George uttered again, doom-laden. Suddenly, their entire plan seemed ruined. Worse than that, this one little mistake would mean they would be discovered. A rumble of distant thunder filled the long silence. "We have to go back," George said. They both leapt up and hurried out, along the stony paths which skirted fields, towards the school.

# Azar

Suddenly, around a bend ahead of them there came a lithe brown horse pulling a two-wheeled cart. On it sat a robust looking man in a grubby white shirt. Emma grabbed George and shoved him back the way they'd come. "It's my uncle," she hissed. "Can't have him see us going to the school." They hurried away from him until they came to a fork in the paths.

"This way," George said. He knew from a childhood of exploration and adventure in these lanes and copses that this path curled around between old buildings and waterways, before leading back to the village and the school. Emma followed, and together they raced along the dry track, shielding their faces from the whip of low-hanging twigs.

"Hey!" There came a shout from a copse around which the path curved. "Hey, you two!"

"Oh no," George said, "it's Stan." They slowed, both realising they couldn't let Stan see them going back to the school.

"George!" Stan called. "New girl!" He hadn't learned her name yet.

"He sounds upset," Emma noticed.

"Come here!" Stan shouted, waving vigorously at them from among a thicket of brambles and bracken.

George and Emma glanced at each other, and began walking towards him. Emma was right though, Stan did sound worried, and he looked it too. They broke into a jog, pushing fronds of bracken aside and stepping over grassy tussocks. Stan had bobbed down out of sight, as if examining something. And then they heard the most awful noise George had ever heard: a long, inhuman yowl of choking pain. "What the devil...?" George said, freezing. "Stan?" He and Emma peered into the gloom of the copse, and thunder clattered across the hills far behind them.

"Hurry up," Stan called urgently, bobbing back up into view. George breathed again, relieved that Stan hadn't been eaten by some unseen monster, but then came another yowl. They scrambled towards him, at last emerging from the undergrowth into a tangled patch of weedy ground. He was kneeling over something long and white and moving.

"Azar?" Emma breathed as they approached.

"I heard him crying," Stan said, looking up through his own tears. "He's stuck in a rabbit trap."

The cat writhed and choked, and the snare

around its neck dug into its skin, a razor sharp noose tightening with every twist of the cat's anguished body.

"Have to get it off," Emma said breathlessly.

"I can't, I've tried," Stan said. George knew what needed to be done. Shaking, he brushed the leaves and soil aside to find the cord which would run from the slip-knot of the snare to a nearby peg. The cord was buried deep – it must have been there a long time. But he dug in the soil, and Stan joined in, until they were able to expose it and follow it with their fingers. The peg had been firmly hammered in, and was hard to move, but between them they managed to yank it this way and that, until at last, it came free. But the cord was still tight around the cat's scrawny neck, and they turned to see Emma using her lockpicks to snag it and loosen the snare. The knot slipped, and Emma widened the loop with her fingers, until she could ease it over the fading cat's head.

The cat, exhausted from its battle, lay on its side, its throat rasping, its ribs rising and falling too quickly.

"Azar," Emma whispered, leaning close to the cat's twitching ear. Straightening up, she said, "I think he's dying."

"We have to take him to my dad," George said. "He's a vet."

# Stan's Tears

Before the war began, George's father had been a busy man, and would very often not be there on a Sunday afternoon. But lately, more and more of the local farmers and villagers were making a point of taking their sick animals to women who had offered their services as vets, or men who were beyond soldiering age, instead of summoning the vet they had long known and trusted. And so, when the three children burst in, he was there in his chair, smoking his pipe and writing a letter.

"Dad!" George panted. "The cat!"

Seeing the panic in their eyes, and listening to their garbled accounts of what had happened, George's father leapt up and took the cat in his arms. Azar seemed alarmed at the whole thing and his claws were out, but he lacked the energy to use them. Besides, George's dad knew exactly how to hold a struggling cat without getting scratched. If George's mother had been there, she'd have soothed the children and maybe given them each a drink of cool milk, but she wasn't, so they bounced and clamoured around the vet as he checked the cat over.

At last, George's dad placed Azar onto the table. The cat sat up weakly, and licked a paw.

"I think he's going to be perfectly alright," George's dad said, smiling as he delivered the welcome news. "There are no permanent injuries." The children's mouths were open wide, and the relief brought tears to the eyes of both Emma and Stan.

Emma wiped hers away. "Stupid cat," she scolded softly. "You should learn to look where you're going."

George was about to introduce Emma, whom his father had never met, but Stan was still crying.

"Um..." George's father said, and everyone looked at each other, not knowing what to say to Stan. So George's father put his arm round the boy's shoulder. "Don't worry, Stan, cats are tough creatures. He's had a shock, but he'll be well again tomorrow, you'll see." But Stan didn't seem to be able to stop crying.

"You saved him, Stan," George said.

"It's..." Stan struggled to get his words out, "... not..." he sniffed and snorted uncontrollably, "... just that," he managed.

"Well what on earth is it then, poor boy?" George's father asked, guiding him to a chair.

"George, please fetch a hanky, and maybe a mug of water." George did as he told, and gradually, Stan began to calm down.

"I... was... sad about the cat..." he began, "but that's not why... I'm crying now."

"Well, then, you must tell us your troubles," George's father said, warmly. "A problem shared is a problem halved, you know." Stan looked a little blank at that.

"He means you'll feel better if you tell us what's wrong," George clarified for him. So Stan, very slowly, began to explain.

"I miss my dad," he said. "He'd know what to do."

"About what?" said George.

"About my mum. She's sad all the time. Really sad. Sometimes she can't even speak. Sometimes she doesn't get out of bed and I have to do everything for her. She just lies there, staring. Sometimes, I think... I think she's died. And at night she cries, and I wake up, and I go and lie in her bed and cuddle her, but I don't know if she likes that. I wish my dad would come home."

George's father asked, "Is your mother sad because your father is away in the war?"

"I think so. My uncle went away too, and he... he won't be coming back." They all knew what that meant.

"I'm terribly sorry to hear that, Stan," George's father said. George and Emma just stood there feeling helpless. On the table, Azar rolled onto his back and stretched. He seemed to be feeling much better already. George placed his hand on Stan's shoulder. He felt deeply sorry for him, and he glanced across at Emma. Was she regretting the trick they'd set up in the school? *He* certainly was. But, he remembered, Stan really did bully him, and would, no doubt, continue to do so. What should they do?

"It's a strange thing, Stan," George's father said: "your mum is sad because your father is away fighting. My wife is sad because I'm not."

A violent crack of thunder rolled across the sky, and rain began to hiss against the lattice windows.

# George and Emma's Dilemma

Later on, George, Emma and Stan were walking back through the wet street. Crisp, clean clouds were breaking above them to reveal blue sky. "I like your dad," Stan said. "He said I can come and play, and have tea, anytime I want."

"I know he did," said George. "Let me know when you're coming, so I can make sure I'm not there."

"Okay," Stan replied, and then realised what George had said. "Hey!" he complained, affronted. They walked on in silence, across town, towards Stan's house. Azar, who seemed much more like his old self now, trotted along behind Emma. "I don't want to go home," Stan said. George and Emma didn't know what to say to that. Stan's life sounded awful, and there was nothing they could do. "Thanks for these though," he added, clutching to his chest the stack of comics George had given him. Sometime later, they arrived at Stan's door. He said a mournful goodbye, then looked down at his comics and brightened again.

"He'll be alright," said George as he and Emma

headed away.

"Well," Emma said, "until tomorrow morning anyway." They looked at each other. "What do we do?" she said, guiltily.

"I don't know. He did dangle me upside down from the hayloft."

"He did. But he did save Azar too, and he ain't very happy. I feel sorry for him."

"It should've been him in the snare," George said, and immediately wished he hadn't. He sighed. "We've got to stop it," he decided.

They both realised that if they were going to do that, they had to get to the school right now, this afternoon. This could not wait until tomorrow morning. So, once again, they ran, this time down wet, muddy lanes where trees and undergrowth relentlessly showered them with cold droplets, as if it was still raining. At last, kneeling beside the back door of the school, Emma opened the satchel that was still slung across her body. She rummaged. She looked up at George. "I ain't got me lockpicks," she confessed. "I had them when we was rescuing Azar. Oh, you stupid cat," she said to the creature which rubbed itself against her. "Look what you done!"

"Well, can't you do it without them?"

"What? How?"

"I don't know," George said, beginning to feel frantic. "Witchcraft?"

Emma ignored that. "We have to go and find them," she said. So they hurried back to the copse where Stan had rescued Azar, but as they got closer, Emma scooped the cat up, and said, "I ain't taking him back there again. He'll get scared. Or... what if there are more snares?" George didn't say anything. He knew she was right, so he went on alone, picking his way through soggy grass and sopping stems. He searched, but he couldn't find the lockpicks. He didn't even know if he was looking in the right place. Under the trees, everywhere looked the same. He kept trying different places, feeling certain he was in the right spot, and then doubting himself and moving with great certainty to a slightly different location. His search was filthy and fruitless.

"Can't find them anywhere," he said returning to the path where Emma stood, Azar at her heels again. He showed Emma his filthy hands. Normally, he might have waved them in her face to try and make her squeal, but this was not the right time, so he washed them in a puddle.

A voice cut through the evening air: "Emma!

Emma! Where are you? Emma! You need to come home. Now!"

"It's my uncle," Emma said. "Sounds serious."

"You can't go!" George pleaded. "What am I going to do?"

"Nothing," Emma said with a shrug. "Go home. You can't stop it now. Besides, like you said, Stan probably still deserves it. He did dangle you from —"

"Emma!" came the voice, closer now.

"I gotta go," she said, and off she and Azar went.

"Wait!" George tried, but she didn't. And it was beginning to rain again.

*

Back at home, George's mind was whirling. What should he do? Could he allow Stan to suffer the cruel fate they had planned? Why had he let Emma talk him into this? And it wasn't just Stan who would suffer. It was Mr Haxby too. Somehow, George wasn't so sure he wanted to see that now either. He was even feeling guilty about that poor hen locked up in the cupboard. He had to stop all this. He weighed up his options: he could let events unfold as planned, and then own up. That way, Stan wouldn't be in trouble, and Mr Haxby would still have had his public humiliation. Or, he could tell Mr Haxby all about it before anything even happened. Yes, that was what he'd do. He'd just have to spend the whole night building up the courage.

# The Threat

He was woken by the crowing of a distant cockerel. He quickly washed and got dressed, and went downstairs. His mother and father were in the kitchen, but something was different: the usual smell of wood-smoke and eggs was not there.

His mother looked at him as he stepped slowly towards them. Something was wrong.

"What?" George said, searching their stern faces for clues. Had they found out his plan?

"George," his mother said, "sit down, love." George did as he was told. "You won't be going to school today."

"Wha...?" They knew. It was written all over their faces.

"We... you and I... are going to stay with Aunt Sarah for a while."

"Mum," George managed, about to blurt out his confession, but his dad sat down beside him and took hold of his hand.

"I'm so sorry it has come to this, George."

"Dad, I..."

"You know things have been very difficult for a

while. You know your mother and I love each other very much, but we can't agree on the issue of conscientious objection. You know what the women in the village think of me." George was confused. What did this have to do with him? "We had a threat from someone. I won't sugarcoat this, George: someone threatened to burn down the cottage."

"Burn it down? Why?"

"So that I would have nowhere to live, and would be forced to go away and fight, I suppose."

His mother took over now: "So, we are going to stay with your aunt for a while. Until your father decides what he is going to do."

"All of us?" George said, although he thought he probably knew the answer to that.

"You and me. Your father will stay here and work things out."

"But... what if they burn the place down?" George said, his voice trembling.

"They don't want to kill me," his father said, "just to drive me out. They'll give me a warning, and someone will need to be here to put out the fire."

"But if you're not here, they won't set fire to it in the first place," George spouted.

"I'm not so sure about that, my boy. These

women are a determined bunch. And if I came to Aunt Sarah's, that might put her in danger too. Do you see? I am fighting war itself, and this is how war fights."

"So," said his mother, "you will go upstairs and put a week's worth of clothes into your bag. We are going to catch the morning train."

"But Mum!"

"George," she said in her dangerous, warning voice, and a lump came to his throat.

"Yes, but, Mum, can't we go tomorrow? I really need to go to school today."

"We are going this morning," his mother said, flatly. "It won't be forever. You will see your school friends again."

"But I have to —"

"You have to do as I say." She made it clear that was her final word. He had no choice.

"Come on," his father said. "I'll help you." Reluctantly, George followed him upstairs. For a few minutes, George sat on his bed watching him opening drawers and piling up shirts and socks and other items of clothing.

George's stomach burned and churned and at last he forced out the words, "I've done something

59

really bad."

"Oh?" his father said, folding a vest and sitting on the bed at George's feet.

"Yes, I have. I'm going to get someone in trouble. I mean, they do deserve it, but... but... I don't want to do it anymore."

"Is it Stan, by any chance?"

"Yes. How did you know?"

"Just a guess. I do know you two sometimes don't get along all that well, and that girl, young Emma, she looks mischievous. I'll bet she's got something to do with it."

"Well, maybe. But... it's not just Stan, Dad. It's Mr Haxby too."

"Tell me."

"I've done something that is going to make him... very embarrassed in front of everyone." He'd opened the floodgates now, and he couldn't stop the words tumbling out. He told his dad exactly what he and Emma had done.

"Well, my boy, you do know that's a terrible thing to do, don't you?" George nodded. "I must say," his father went on, "I'm very surprised. After all the things you've heard people say to me about not going to war, and you want to do that to Mr Haxby? Do you know the real reason he's refusing to go to war?" George shook his head. "Mr Haxby has a very sick wife. I don't know exactly what's wrong with her, but she's been ill for years, and only gets worse."

"Is she dying?"

"Possibly, I don't know. But Mr Haxby... He's never been a popular chap. I'm not sure he even has any true friends, and that might be his own fault: he can be cantankerous and sharp with people. But he loves his wife, and is dedicated to her happiness. There is no-one else to look after her. I happen to know this because he has a horse, and he is one of the few people left who is still happy to use my veterinary services, and sometimes he does get chatting. He would love to go to war, to fight for king and country, but he cannot, because he can't leave his wife alone. And, whatever else you might think of him, he's no coward. Think about your history lessons. Mr Haxby is a little older than me." George looked blankly at his father. "The Boer War, my boy, was a terrible thing. He fought in that war. He was too young, actually, but lied about his age so that the army would let him join. Afterwards, he left the army to care for his wife. I don't think he ever really wanted to be a teacher, but that's where life led him. So, yes, he might be a strict and frightening teacher. You might think he is unfair sometimes, but I know you find it hard to keep quiet in the classroom, George, don't you?" George had to admit that he did. "I was just like you. Boys like us often think their teachers are unfair. But today, my boy, I think you are the one who is being unfair."

George felt worse than ever. He was a terrible person. And now his dad could see that too. He felt as if his shame was going to swell inside him and split him apart like an overripe tomato. "Dad, I have to get to school. I can stop it, but you have to let me go. Otherwise I'll be too late."

"Indeed you do," his father agreed.

Together, they went downstairs again.

"Are you packed?" George's mother said.

"My dear," his dad said.

"No, don't you 'my dear' me," his mother said, rising from her seat and filling the room with her threatening tone. "Don't you dare stand against me on this. We are going, and we are going *now*."

"You must let him do something first," his dad said softly and warmly.

"George," his mother snapped, "get your case. Is it packed? We have a train to catch."

"Why?" George objected, petulantly.

"Because I told you to."

"Love, there isn't time to explain," his father said. "You must let him go."

"What on earth's going on?" his mother said, her fury suddenly giving way to concern. "Are you alright, George?"

"Mum, I have to do something," George said, but found himself rooted to the spot.

"Lizzie," his dad said, putting his hands on his wife's shoulders. "Let him go. I'll explain."

At first, anger flashed across her face again, but then her expression softened, and she nodded. "Very well," she said. "Off you go."

# In Front Of The

# Whole School

George ran the full length of the village, past the trundling milk cart, past the bakers, past the village hall where Union Jack bunting waved in the breeze, and he kept running, until his legs burned and his lungs felt full of hot sand. At last the school came into view. He wasn't sure what time it was, but the old sundial on the school wall showed he was already too late.

He hurtled inside. All he could do now was hope that Emma had got there ahead of him and put a stop to things. Breathless, he arrived in the main hall, just as the last few children were sitting themselves down, ready for assembly to begin. Miss May, the church organist who always came to play the hymn, was perched on the piano stool, and Mr Haxby was at the front, glaring at anyone who dared to fidget.

George stood there, gasping for breath, wondering what on earth to do. Mr Haxby looked at him, and said, "Sanders, what are you doing?"

"I..."

"Well, come on boy, get yourself together. You are late for school. Don't loiter there. Come and sit down."

George edged closer, knowing he had to say something right now, or the chance would be lost forever. Mr Haxby was already heading towards the cupboard. George scanned the room for Emma, but couldn't see her. He could see Stan though, looking round at him and grinning in greeting. He even gave George an innocent little wave. Mr Haxby was reaching in his pocket for his keys, jangling them as he pulled them out, searching the bunch for the cupboard key.

"Wait!" George shouted.

"Sit down, Sanders," Mr Haxby commanded.

"Don't open the cupboard!" Everyone had turned to look at him now, and he could feel his face burning up.

"Why ever not, boy?" Mr Haxby enquired. Miss May, sensing a problem, stood, as if getting ready to catch a ball.

"I..." George did not know what to say. "Please, Sir, can I talk to you... privately?"

"Now? Of course not. Can't you see I'm about to

65

take an assembly?" And with that, Mr Haxby thrust the key into the lock.

"No!" George blurted, lurching towards him. "Don't!"

A wave of startled and curious whispers flowed across the hall.

"Silence!" Mr Haxby barked. "Miss May, could you please take this raving lunatic out and find out what ails him?"

"Certainly, Mr Haxby," Miss May said, and strode towards George.

Mr Haxby turned the key, and found the door was stuck.

"Come with me, George," Miss May commanded.

Mr Haxby gave the cupboard door a firm shake. "Why won't it open?" George heard him breathe. Then, they all heard the unmistakable squawking of an agitated hen coming from within the cupboard. Another murmur of noise bubbled up from the children.

Miss May shushed them, and repeated her command, but George, arriving now at the cupboard, put his hands on Mr Haxby's, and looked up at him. "Don't open it," he implored. Mr Haxby returned his gaze, his small green eyes full of confusion, and paused in his efforts. George could hear him breathing, and smell the bitter sting of his breath. In the cupboard, the hen clucked and flapped. In the hall, the children fell into a silence of eager anticipation. George could see Stan, his wide eyes watching the scene, enthralled.

"Come on," Miss May said in her fiercest voice, her hand on George's arm now. She gave him a firm tug, pulling him off balance, away from Mr Haxby. George took a few stumbling steps as Miss May pulled him towards the door before he shook his arm free and turned back to Mr Haxby, but he was too late. A final yank of the cupboard door brought it swinging open and out came the blinding, flapping, flurry of feathers. Mr Haxby stepped back in alarm, and the hen blustered past his face, depositing whirling white feathers into the air. The children roared in delight, moving backwards like a receding wave, and Mr Haxby and Miss May bellowed at them to be still. Then, one of the older children pointed.

Mr Haxby's eyes followed the gaze of the children until he saw the insult on the inside of the cupboard door which now stood wide, like a billboard. Some of the children were laughing. Some

67

were sitting in stunned silence. Feathers fell around Mr Haxby, and the agitated hen settled on the gymnastics box. Mr Haxby's face had taken on an expression George had never seen before. His cheeks were red, his mouth was open and his eyes were wide. Then, surprisingly calmly, he said to Miss May, "Could you please take over the assembly?" And, to George, he said, "Sanders, follow me."

# An Almighty Thrashing

Mr Haxby's office was spacious and bright. At one end was a high, arched window which flooded the room with light. Mr Haxby, sitting at his desk, turning a pen over and over in his fingers, was almost a silhouette against the window, but George could feel his sharp eyes glaring at him. George did not know where to look. On either side of George sat his parents, and from high up on a shelf, Snowy looked on, crossly.

"I really don't know where to start," Mr Haxby said, after a long and painful silence. "George's behaviour is utterly unacceptable. Quite appalling."

"I couldn't agree more," George's father said.

"Indeed," said his mother.

Snowy clucked.

"The question is," Mr Haxby went on, "what do we do about it? Mr Sanders, I would have happily expelled any other child, but since we are friends..." George knew that was stretching things a bit. "...And also in the light of the fact that the boy did try to prevent me from opening the cupboard, I will not expel him."

"Thank you," George's father said.

"Thank you, Mr Haxby," George said, meekly.

"Rest assured," his mother interjected, "he will be severely punished."

Turning towards George, Mr Haxby said, "I won't expel you, but you do know you are in for an almighty thrashing, boy, don't you?"

George swallowed hard. Mr Haxby had caned him for lesser crimes several times before, and that was bad enough, but the thought of an 'almighty thrashing' terrified him. Beside him, his mother was nodding in agreement with Mr Haxby, so George looked up at his father instead. Surely he would not let this happen. His father's face was hard to read. George could see he was undecided. Mr Haxby was silent, waiting for his response. George's father stood, paced across the room and back again. He looked up at Snowy, as if she might have the answer. Perhaps she did, because he gave her a nod and sat back down decisively.

Looking at George, he said, "My son, I abhor the violence of war, as you know. But this is not war. This is punishment. You've committed an offence and so you must accept the punishment bravely."

George blinked. He opened his mouth to object,

but closed it again and nodded.

"George," Mr Haxby said, "the trick you played was... *vile*. How could you do such a thing, not just to me, but to your friend Stan too?"

Snowy clucked, and flapped her wings, as if to remind them who the real victim was.

"I know, I'm really sorry," George managed.

"He does know that what he wrote about you was not true," his father said. "That's why he tried to stop it."

"Yes," said Mr Haxby, "but the rest of the school does not know that."

"I'll... I'll... I'll tell them," George stammered.

"Do I seem like a man who cares what other people think of him, George? It does not interest me whether or not they think me a coward. What interests me is that the children work hard, and do well. But now I fear they may be less inclined to do so, as their respect for me will be undermined. I hope you can grasp the enormity of what you have done, not to me, but to them and their education."

Surprised, George nodded and wiped his eyes.

Tell me," Mr Haxby said, "whose idea was it? Please don't say you were acting alone."

"I was," George lied. "It was just me. I found the

hen in the woods. She must have escaped." He suddenly remembered his father knew Emma was involved, and he glanced up at him guiltily. His father returned the glance, and then said to Mr Haxby, "I'll ask around. I can probably find out who's missing a hen."

"How on earth did you get in to the school?" Mr Haxby asked.

"Um..." that was a good question. George had no idea how to get out of this. "The classroom window was open," he said, plucking the answer out of the air. His vision was frosted by a thick film of hot tears now, and his throat was bursting with the effort of keeping himself from crying. He said, in a quiet, wobbly voice, "I'm really sorry, Mr Haxby."

"Hmmm," Mr Haxby replied, and his green eyes narrowed. But, strangely, he didn't seem angry. Just perplexed, a little like Stan whenever George said anything mean to him.

\*

George's father returned Snowy to Emma's uncle, and somehow did it without raising his suspicions about Emma's involvement. The very next day George's mother took him away to Aunt Sarah's large country house where she proceeded to teach him herself for the rest of that week and two more after that too, so in effect, he was temporarily expelled from school. Mr Haxby had given him several hard whacks with the cane, and when he had finished, George's mother had taken the cane and given him two more. She'd also made George offer to go to Mr Haxby's house in his spare time and help with jobs like gardening and doing the laundry. George hated the idea, but secretly felt it was a fair punishment. That would have to wait until they came back home though.

While they were away, no-one burned the cottage down. George and his father wrote to each other several times, and his father even came to stay at Aunt Sarah's for one night. George overheard his mother, in the drawing room just after breakfast, saying to his father, "I do love you, and respect you. I understand why you won't go and fight. And, even though I do think you *should* go, I do not *want* you to. I would hate for you to get hurt."

George's father received no more threats, and it seemed that the danger of the cottage being burnt down had passed, so, George and his mother returned home. But that very afternoon, George overheard another conversation between his parents:

"It's the law," his father said. "I've been called up." George knew what that meant. Joining the army used to be voluntary, even though everyone in the village seemed to think it was your duty to volunteer and you were a coward if you didn't. But the government had recently introduced conscription, meaning you could be called up, and then you would have to join the fighting whether you liked it or not. "If I continue to refuse, I could be put in prison. What should I do, my love?"

There was a silence, and George tried to imagine what his mother was thinking. Surely she would tell him he definitely had to go and join the fighting now. But, to his surprise, she said tenderly, "I think... you should hold true to your principles. You must stand your ground."

# Emma's Lie

That evening, George went searching for Emma. The last time he'd seen her was the day when Stan had saved Azar. He knew where to look. He waited in the barn, and listened to the slow, heavy drumming of rain on the tin roof. He lay there in the old cart for what must have been hours, dozing, until a sudden scream from only an arm's length away almost made his heart fly out of his chest. He sat bolt upright, and was flooded with relief when he heard the sound of Emma laughing.

"You frightened me half to death!" George said, smiling.

"Hah! Sorry. Couldn't resist it!" Emma replied. "So, you're back then. I thought I'd never see you again," she grinned, pulling a brown leaf out of her tangled hair. "Thought they'd sent you away forever!"

"It felt as if they had," George said. "Uh, it was *sooooo booooooring* at Aunt Sarah's! And I've got to help Mr Haxby dig his garden and do his washing and things, as an apology. Ugh, I bet I have to scrub his *pants* with my bare hands!" They both laughed.

"S'pose I should come and help you really,"

Emma said, and Azar meowed for attention.

"Would you?"

"Depends on if I'm bored, and if my uncle has chores for me to do. Thanks though," Emma added, throwing Azar up onto the cart and clambering onto it herself.

"What for?"

"For not telling them I was involved. I'd have been expelled, quick as lightning. We don't all have your *favourable connections*," she said in a pretend posh voice.

"Shut up!" George objected. "What happened to you, anyway? You weren't there at school that day."

"I know. Wish I had been. I'd have loved to see what happened!"

"You wouldn't, it was terrible. I wanted to die. So, where were you? Was everything alright?"

"Well... I suppose I should tell you. I do owe you one." She stroked Azar, and for a while George thought she wasn't going to tell him anything after all. But she did. "You know I told you my dad was a soldier, fighting in the war?" George nodded. "Well, he ain't. He's in prison."

"Oh," George said. "My dad might be going to prison too. Is your dad a pacifist after all then?"

"Nope. He's a thief. He robbed the houses of soldiers who was away fighting. We had to run away here to escape from the police. My uncle let us stay. But, that night, the police had come and taken my dad to prison. That's why my uncle came calling me."

"Oh," George breathed, awestruck.

"So you see," Emma said, "your dad don't seem so shameful now, does he?"

"No," George said, and then realised he shouldn't have. "Sorry."

"Don't be," Emma said. "He's a useless father. He's never cared about me, and I've never cared about him."

George reflected that she'd said something similar about her mum. And she always made out that she didn't like Azar too, but she clearly did.

"I won't tell anyone about your dad," George assured her.

"Tell who you like," she said. "It doesn't matter anymore. If anyone says anything to me, I'll just punch 'em."

George laughed again. "You're a bit like my mum!"

"Anyway," Emma said. "At least I know something now."

"Oh? What's that then?"

"You're not a *complete* coward."

"Thanks, I think," said George. "Have you seen Stan at all? I really want to apologise to him."

"Apologise to *him*?" Emma gasped. "What for? He deserved everything he *nearly* got! What you gonna do next time he tries to bully you into doing his homework for him?"

"I've been thinking about that," said George. "I've had a lot of time to think about it. If Stan tries to get me to do his homework, I think I'll tell him 'no', but I will help him with it if he wants."

"Oh, you're such a coward!" Emma teased. "I knew there was a reason I didn't like you!"

"But," George went on, "if he doesn't accept my offer of help, I'll punch him."

"That's more like it," Emma said. "Have you ever punched anyone before though?"

"Nope."

"Well, don't worry," she said. "I'll teach you. Come on!"

# Mr Haxby's Wife

"Oi, you two, wait!" It was Stan, and he was already running down the lane towards them, splashing through puddles as if they didn't even exist. Before they could take evasive action, he was upon them. The first thing he did was to bend over and pick up Azar, hoisting the delighted cat onto his shoulders and laughing as the creature curled itself round the back of his head. Leaning forward so that Azar could make his leisurely way down his back, Stan said, "What you two up to?"

"Got to go and dig Mr Haxby's garden," George informed him.

"Really? Why?"

"Because of what I did."

"What did you do?"

George looked at him as if to say, 'what do you think?' but Stan was too busy trying to look at the cat on his back to notice. Emma lifted Azar off him and deposited the creature on the muddy path.

"You know," George reminded him.

"Oh," Stan remembered. "Fair enough I suppose. Hey, it wasn't just Mr Haxby you were mean to. Are you going to dig *my* garden too?" he grinned. George thought that was pretty insightful for Stan, and he grinned back.

"No," he said, "but..." and he took a breath, building himself up for his big apology. "I'm..." He glanced at Emma; she gave him an encouraging nod. "I'm really sorry, Stan," George finished.

"Why? What for?"

Again, George just looked at him. "You mentioned it yourself ten seconds ago!" George said at last. "I tried to set you up, remember? You do know it was a big plan to get you in trouble?"

"Yes, obviously," Stan retorted. "But it doesn't matter coz I made you do my homework lots of times, so we're quits now. Haxby caned me for that, by the way, so thanks for telling, tell-tale! Anyway, he's been tutoring me at his house, so I can do long-multiplication now, a bit, so you won't have to do it for me anymore."

Emma chuckled at that.

"Stan," George said. "I will never do your homework for you ever again. Do you get that?"

Stan looked a bit hurt, but then said, with a note of resignation, "Okay." Turning left, he said, "Come on, Haxby's house is this way."

"It's this way," George corrected him, turning right.

Mr Haxby's house was some way out of the village. George had never been there, but his mother had given him the directions, and it was quite easy to find. It was a small, detached, brick building with tall chimneys and ivy engulfing at least half of it. It was surrounded by an expanse of garden, dotted with trees and bushes, rockeries and flower beds. As George opened the gate, he felt as if he was walking into the den of a very hungry lion. Cautiously, he led the way towards the house, looking around as their feet crunched on the gravel path.

"Ah, there you are, Sanders," came Mr Haxby's voice, just before they reached the steps to the front door. They all turned round to see their teacher coming towards them across the grass.

"Here we go," George whispered.

Behind Mr Haxby, they could see an old lady in a wicker wheelchair, a blanket over her knees, her head bowed as if she was asleep.

"Who's she?" Emma whispered to George, who shrugged in reply.

"I see you've brought your entourage with you, Sanders," Mr Haxby said. "I'd really prefer it if your cat doesn't foul the lawn. If he does, I would ask you to clear it up right away. There's a trowel in the shed. Thank you so much for coming. It will be a great help to have you here." George, who had not seen Mr Haxby since that awful day in his office, had been bracing himself for another telling off, and had half expected Emma and Stan to be sent home. But Mr Haxby seemed almost pleased to see them. He didn't actually smile, but something about his manner made him seem a little less fearsome and distant than usual. Maybe it was because he wasn't wearing the black gown he wore in school, that made him look like a bat. Today he was wearing wellington boots and dungarees, and his hair was not as neat and preened as usual. He also wasn't wearing his glasses. It made his eyes look smaller, but somehow brighter too.

"Bring them over," called the old lady, her head still drooping forward but was now turned awkwardly towards them. "Bring them over," came her sharp, shaky voice, but Stan was already bounding across the lawn towards her.

"Hello, Mrs Haxby!" Stan called.

"Hello, Stanley," she replied, in her odd croak.

"Is it his mother?" Emma suggested quietly to

# Chapter 14: Mr Haxby's Wife

George.

"Must be." George felt himself shudder: he didn't want to meet this crabby, wizened old woman. She looked like the wicked witch from a fairy tale. She would know all about Mr Haxby's humiliation in the assembly, and she'd know George was responsible.

George, Emma and Azar followed Stan and Mr Haxby across the lawn. "She's going to kill me," George whispered.

"Well, she might not actually *kill* you," Emma reassured him, "but I wouldn't be surprised if she turns you into a frog."

Mr Haxby introduced them. To George's surprise, the old woman was actually Mr Haxby's wife. She seemed to have great difficulty raising her head, but she looked up at them in turn through her stringy eyebrows. "I do know," she said, in her slow, laboured voice, "exactly what you did."

"That's enough, my love," Mr Haxby said, laying his hand on her shoulder. "No need to bring that up now, it's all done and dusted."

"Indeed. But I'd like the children to know that I do know all about it. I know what you did, George, and I doubt he did it on his own, Emma." Emma looked very uneasy, and shifted her feet awkwardly in the grass. "And Stan, you know I know about you and your homework. And I also know that my husband can be a cold and overly strict teacher."

"Dearest..." Mr Haxby tried, but his wife shushed him sharply. And then she laughed, softly, into her chest.

"So there we have it. It's all out in the open, and it's all forgotten. Now, husband, please fetch some sustenance for these minions of yours. You can't expect them to dig the vegetable patch without a lovely big chunk of cake inside them." Then, she began to heave herself out of her wheelchair. Mr Haxby stepped forward to help her, but she waved him away. "He thinks I'm an invalid," she informed the children. "Cake, my love," she reminded Mr Haxby, who, reluctantly, turned and headed towards the house.

Mrs Haxby very clearly was an invalid, but George saw how determined she was to get up and walk about. She used a stick, and she seemed happy to let Stan support her by holding her arm; he'd clearly done that before. In fact, she and Stan seemed to be very well acquainted. She walked in a slow, painful shuffle, but made no complaint whatsoever.

She showed them around the garden, and proved to be jolly and cheerful. The more she spoke to them, the more George realised she wasn't an old woman after all, but someone around the same age as his mother, who clearly had a disease that made her life very hard.

Throughout the day, the children did do some work in the garden, but most of their time was spent sitting on a blanket on the damp grass listening to Mrs Haxby's stories. She had, it seemed, a wild past of mischief-making and hell raising, back in Africa where she had grown up. Always in trouble with her parents, teachers and the local vicar, at the age of sixteen she'd fallen in love with a handsome young soldier from England, one who had lied about his age so he could come and fight in the Boer War. She'd married him, and become Mrs Haxby.

As she recounted the tales of her past, making the children laugh and gasp and cheer, she seemed to George to become less and less old and disabled, until he didn't see her illness anymore, just her happy, excited eccentricities. She was a young woman, full of energy and fun. Mr Haxby sat on a deck chair, just listening, and smiling.

# Fire!

At last, the sun began to dip, and the air grew cold. It was time to go.

"I'll take you back," Mr Haxby said, "to make sure you don't get into any trouble." It was the sort of thing he would normally say, but somehow, George sensed he was joking this time. He disappeared to ready the horse and cart, both of which resided in a small paddock behind the house. A few minutes later he reappeared, driving the cart along the road to the front gate. Mrs Haxby stubbornly hobbled up the path to wave them off. As Mr Haxby helped the children up into the cart, George could not believe he was actually looking forward to coming back to his teacher's house to do chores! He felt as if everything was alright again: he'd been filled with guilt for what he'd done to Stan and Mr Haxby, but Mrs Haxby had brought all that out into the open and made it seem insignificant. He'd even forgotten about the threat of prison hanging over his dad.

They bounced along, Azar sitting proudly between Stan and Emma, and Mr Haxby began to reminisce. All afternoon his wife had done most of the talking, but now he began to tell them about Africa. He didn't talk about the war he'd been in. Instead he talked about hills and valleys and glorious sunsets. He talked about how lovely his wife had been: young and pretty, and devilishly funny. George realised that just as Mrs Haxby had been very different back then, Mr Haxby must have been too.

Twilight was closing in as they arrived at the village, but as they approached they saw an ominous, orange glow in the sky. Sparks rose, and dark smoke curled upwards from somewhere behind the nearest houses.

Mr Haxby looked as if he didn't know what to say.

"Where's it coming from?" Emma asked.

"Is it...?" George began, but his throat knotted up.

Stan said, "It looks as if it's coming from George's house!"

Mr Haxby gave the reins a shake and the horse sped up, making the cart lurch. They rounded the corner into the lane where George lived, and sure enough, it was his house the flames were coming from. Terror filled him. Half of the thatch was engulfed in fire. In front of the house stood a crowd of onlookers. They didn't seem to be doing anything, just watching.

"You children, wait here," Mr Haxby said, pulling on the brake. But George hardly heard him. He jumped down from the cart, and forced his way through the crowd.

There stood his mother, desperation on her face. George realised she was helpless. She couldn't tackle the blaze on her own, and she was begging the onlookers for help. He felt sick; he'd never seen her like this; she was normally in control of everything. When she saw George, she grabbed him and pulled him to her.

"Where's Dad?" George cried.

"He's safe; he's gone away."

"*Run* away, more like," one of the women suggested. It was Mrs Pemberton, the butcher's wife. George saw that the crowd was made up of women and a few older men.

"No, he has not run away. He is no coward. Won't someone go for the fire brigade?"

"Someone already called 'em," Mrs Pemberton said calmly. "We're not monsters, Liz. They'll be a while though. All the men are away fighting a war."

"You disgust me," George's mother hissed at the

crowd. "This is far worse than handing out feathers. This is our *home*, my *son's* home."

"It weren't the women who started the fire," said a gruff male voice, and a man stepped forward. George recognised him as Mr Roe; he was the grandfather of Maggie, the girl who had delivered the feather to his father. "'Twas I, Liz. It's about time that husband o' yours faced up to his duty. His friends and family are out there dyin' in the trenches like my grandson, and what's 'e doing? Won't even go to France as a veterinary. Lord knows they need 'em out there. He's abandoned his fellow man, Liz. It's shameful. Well he'll 'ave to go now, won't 'e?"

"No!" George suddenly shouted. "My dad's a good man! He's fighting *war itself*!"

"Grandfather," came the voice of a young woman who was elbowing her way to the front. "This is awful! We can't let their house burn down!" It was Maggie. "This ain't what Joe would have wanted."

Suddenly, bobbing its way through the crowd like a creature nosing through tall grass, there emerged the end of a ladder. Mr Haxby soon appeared; the ladder was over his shoulder, and behind him Emma had the other end. "Out of the way," Mr Haxby roared. "Out of the way!"

"Hey, that's mine!" someone called.

Ignoring the complaint, Mr Haxby leant the ladder against the house. At that moment, Stan came blustering through the crowd lugging a huge bucket of water which sloshed itself this way and that. Mr Haxby grabbed it from him and shot up the ladder with it. He threw it onto the leading edge of the fire's onslaught. There was a loud hiss and the night air filled with steam. But it would take many, many more of those to extinguish this fire. Emma and Stan had already gone again. A moment later Azar appeared, meowed, and vanished back through the crowd in search of Emma. George shot off after him. Buckets were fairly easy to find in neighbouring gardens around the village green. They weren't all waterproof though, some were only good for holding chicken feed, but soon, George had a couple and was heading for the pond. He passed Emma and Stan who were staggering towards the house, each struggling with a heavy, leaky bucket. George's mother was beside him now, two empty buckets swinging as she ran. And someone overtook them both, her skirts flapping about her like the sails of a ship. It was Maggie. She reached the pond and sank two buckets in the water, filling them instantly, then sped back up the slope towards the house.

George and his mother filled theirs, and heaved them up the slope, across the road, through what was left of the crowd, and placed them at the bottom of the ladder. Mr Haxby was rushing up and down, dumping water on the fire and dropping the empty buckets on the ground for others to refill. Several of the women from the crowd had joined in, and a stream of people was beginning to form between the cottage and the pond. Someone handed him a rake, and he began pulling thatch down to create a fire break.

But Mr Roe stepped out of the darkness and blocked the path of George and his mother.

"Where is he then, this 'usband of yours?" He demanded. "If he's such a brave man, where is he when 'is family needs 'im? Eh?"

"Leave it, Samuel," one of the women warned him, as she waddled past with two unwieldy buckets.

"You're a fool, Mr Roe," George's mother said. "It was his tribunal today. He's gone to prison for his beliefs. And if there were more men like him, the world would be a better place and your grandson would still be alive."

"Mum?" George said, hoping he hadn't heard

her correctly.

"So all this," his mother went on, stepping towards Mr Roe and pointing an accusing finger in his face, forcing him to take a step back, "this fire you started... was for nothing. And I'll make sure you go to prison for it."

Then George heard a rumble of hooves and the frantic clatter of a bell: the fire engine was approaching.

# The Pact

Emma and George were sitting on the edge of the cart, their legs swinging lazily. The barn creaked in the wind around them, and George was twirling a feather in his fingers. It was one of his father's: he'd recovered it when he and his mother had gone back into the house the day after the fire to see what they could salvage. It wasn't white anymore though; the smoke had turned it a blotchy brown.

"Thought you'd want to forget about those feathers," Emma said.

"Well..." George thought for a moment. "It just makes me... question myself," he finished, repeating his father's words.

"You're it!" Stan laughed, slapping George's arm and running backwards away from him.

"Stan!" Emma reprimanded.

"I don't really feel like playing, Stan," George said. "I just don't feel... great."

"Oh," Stan said. "Okay."

"His dad's gone to prison," Emma reminded Stan, "and his house is a wreck."

"Yes, but it's all going to be alright, isn't it?"

Stan said, returning towards them, hands in pockets now. He sat on the floor, and Azar jumped down from the cart. "I mean, Mr Haxby's house is nice. You've got a bigger room now than you had before. Emma's dad's in prison too, and she's not moaning."

"My dad deserved it," said Emma.

"Yeah, but you do miss him, don't you?" Stan said. Emma just looked away. "At least your dads are safe," Stan went on. "Mine's away fighting in the war."

That was true. Poor Stan. "How's your mum, Stan?" George asked, suddenly wishing he'd thought to ask before now.

"Oh, she's... Sometimes she seems okay. She cries a lot. Hey, I got this letter, from my dad. Could you read it for me? His writing's all spidery. You're good at reading adults' writing." He pulled a crumpled piece of paper from his pocket and unfolded it.

"Give it here then," George said, and Stan passed the letter up to him. With the feather still between his fingers, George straightened the letter out and looked it over, clearing his throat as if he was about to deliver an important speech. Emma peered at it, but George angled it away from her, and said,

"Do you mind?"

"Sorry, Sir," Emma retorted, pretending she'd been told off by a teacher.

"Dear Stanley," George began. Stan was so agog that he'd even stopped stroking Azar, and the cat meowed crossly. "I regret to inform you that you have been a very naughty boy and I have arranged for you to be caned mercilessly by Mr Haxby." George, grinning, lowered the letter and looked down at Stan, whose mouth was open and eyes were wide.

"He's joking, Stan," Emma informed him. "Read it properly, you bully," she said, giving George a mighty shove.

"Oh!" Stan said, and smiled. "You idiot!"

"*You* idiot," George said, and then began to read what the letter actually said. "Dear Stan and Rosemary —"

"That's my mum's name," Stan announced.

George resisted the urge to say something sarcastic, like, 'Really? And I thought your mum was called Bernard,' and continued reading: "Life out here is pretty tough, I won't lie to you. But you mustn't worry about me. It can be a bit scary, but the lads are great, and we help each other through. The trenches aren't very nice, and I miss you both very much. I wish you would write more often. Your last letter was over two weeks ago, Rose, and it was very short. That makes me worried. Are you well? I hope you and Stan are looking after each other. You are the ones we are fighting to protect." Stan sniffed. George went on: "You mustn't worry about me. I've made some great friends. Some of the lads have trench foot. That's not nice, but we are up to our ankles in water most of the time. I'm okay though, I seem to have feet of iron! No, perhaps not iron, that would rust. I've got feet of steel! You'd love the rats here, Stan. I'd bring one home for you to have as a pet if I could!" Stan sniffed again, and made a tiny, stifled sound.

"He's crying," Emma whispered.

George looked down at Stan kneeling in the straw, Azar sitting patiently beside him. Emma was right. Stan wiped his nose on the back of his hand, and George jumped down off the cart. "Um..." George said. "It's alright, Stan. He seems really... happy."

"No he doesn't," said Stan, and George realised that for all Stan's inability to understand what was going on half the time, he knew perfectly well what his dad was trying *not* to tell him. George sat on the floor next to Stan, and began to stroke Azar. "Dad hates it there, and he's scared. I can tell," Stan said. George thought about his own father, in prison now for refusing to go to war. He understood why people called him a coward. But George and his mother would be able to go and see him, and no-one was shooting at him, unlike poor Stan's father. But still, George loved his father, and already missed him desperately. He was suddenly overwhelmed with his own sorrow.

"Damn cat," George said, as his eyes filled with tears. "Making my eyes water." He wished he would sneeze, to prove it was his allergies, and that he wasn't really crying. But he didn't sneeze, and the tears kept coming.

Emma jumped down from the cart, and snatched the letter. "Gimme that, you two cry-babies," she said. She began to read the rest of the letter, but George found his mind wandering. The thought of his dad in prison, hated by so many people, made him feel sick. George knew his dad was a kind, good man, and not a coward, but the rest of the world could not see that, except for his mother. And except for Mr and Mrs Haxby. After the fire, they had insisted that George and his mother come and live with them. And just when George was beginning to like Mr Haxby, he'd announced he had been called up. That meant he had to go and fight in the war. He had no choice now, unless he wanted to end up in prison too. But the good thing was, Mr Haxby knew his wife would be looked after while he was away. George and his mother would see to that.

Emma had stopped reading, even though she hadn't come to the end of the letter. George looked up at her. She was blinking heavily, and then she turned her back on the boys. She took a couple of sharp in-breaths and her shoulders bounced up and down.

George rubbed his own tears away and looked at Stan. "She's crying," George said. He stood up, and Stan stood beside him. "What a bunch we are!" George observed, "all of us crying like this!"

"I'm not crying," Stan objected, wiping away another large tear from his cheek.

"Neither... am... I..." Emma managed, between sobs.

"Well, I am," George confessed.

"Me too," Emma said, turning her tear-streaked face towards them.

Stan nodded, and smiled. "I am," he said.

Without another word, they all hugged each

other in a group huddle, and their tears fell to the dusty floor as Azar wound himself around their ankles in turn.

"Well," George said, "we can't stop the war."

"And we can't stop our parents being idiots," Emma said.

"And we can't make them come home, because if they do they'll get shot for desertion," Stan said.

"But we can look after each other," George pointed out.

"Will you help me write to my dad?" Stan asked, as they moved apart again.

"If I say no, are you going to dangle me from the hayloft?"

"Oh, go on," Emma encouraged. "That was so funny!"

"Shut up, you," George retorted.

Stan laughed. Then he said, "No. I reckon you'd punch me if I tried that again anyway."

"Alright then," George said. "We'll help you write to your dad. But first, we need to make a pact. Um..." He looked down at the feather in his hand. "Right, we'll swear on this. Come on."

"It's all grubby," Emma observed.

"I can't help that," George said. He closed his

fingers around it, held out his fist, and the other two placed their hands on top.

"Right, now, um..."

"We can be the Grubby Feather Gang!" Stan interrupted excitedly.

"The Grubby Feather Gang?" George said. Then he and Emma smiled at the idea. "Alright!" they agreed.

"Get on with it then," Emma grinned. "I don't want to stand 'ere looking at your two ugly mugs any longer than I have to!"

"Um... Say this after me," George commanded. "I do solemnly declare..."

"I do solemnly declare," Stan and Emma repeated.

"...That we three friends, hereafter known as the Grubby Feather Gang, will always be there for each other, whatever happens to any of us, and we will always help each other with the problems we have to face." And then he added, "Forever."

There was a silence. "I can't remember all that," said Stan.

"It is a bit long," Emma agreed.

"Oh," George said, deflated. "Alright, I'll say it again, in shorter bits." There was a pause. "I can't remember what I said," he admitted.

"You said," Emma reminded him, "that we three friends —"

"No, that we three *will be* friends forever," Stan said.

"Oh yes, that's much better," George beamed.

So, together, they just said, "That we three will be friends forever." Then, the three members of the newly formed Grubby Feather Gang shook hands vigorously, until they were all laughing uncontrollably. They fell to the floor, laughing until tears flowed once again.

Azar sat on the cart watching them, and licking his paws.

"We should have said, 'we *four* friends!'" Stan suddenly realised. "We forgot Azar!"

"I'm not saying it again," Emma complained, "just for that daft, mangy creature." But she didn't take much persuading.

# Author's Note

The Grubby Feather Gang is a work of fiction. George, Emma and Stan are made up, but the story is based on real historical events. The first world war, also called The Great War, took place during a time of technological change. Swords, cannons and horseback charges were used in the fighting, but so were tanks, zeppelins, aeroplanes and machine guns. Soldiers dug trenches for protection, which in previous wars had proved effective against charging infantry (soldiers on foot) and cavalry (soldiers on horseback), but were no match for tanks.

It must have been a terrifying place to be. If you refused to go, you could be branded a coward. But many men refused because they were opposed to war, just like George's father. These men were called conscientious objectors, or 'conchies' for short.

White feathers had long been seen as a symbol of cowardice – you might have thought I'd made that up for the story, but it is true – and young women often did present them to conchies.

When the war began, men did not *have to* join the army. Many did though, voluntarily, and there was a lot of pressure on them to do so. But in 1916, the law changed, and conscription was brought in, meaning that men no longer had the choice. A conscientious objector would have to face a tribunal, which is much like going to court, to judge whether they really were a conchie or were just pretending to be so that they could escape conscription. Even the real conchies were sent to support the army in France though, helping the wounded without actually fighting. But prison awaited any who refused to go, conchie or not. I've not gone into the details in the story, but that's what happened to George's father. He was one of the few who refused to take part, even in a non-combative role.

So, here's a difficult question: was George's father a coward? You probably already know how difficult it can be to stick to your principles when all of your friends want you to do something which you don't think is right. I'm not asking whether you think George's father was right to become a conscientious objector. I'm asking whether or not you think *sticking to that decision* was an act of cowardice, or an act of bravery.

**BigShorts** are short novels for strong readers, written by Antony Wootten.

## Season of the Mammoth (a BigShorts book)

Trouble is brewing in the tribe. The people are divided. Some want to go to war against the wanderers who travel to their valley every year to hunt mammoths, but others see that the wanderers are dying out and need help. Geb and Tannash, the son and daughter of the tribal leader, along with their reclusive friend, Scrim, are caught in the middle as the tribe splits apart and turns on itself. Can they – *should* they – help defend the wanderers?

## Also by Antony Wootten

## Grown-ups Can't Be Friends With Dragons

Brian is always in trouble at school, and his home life is far from peaceful. So he often runs away to the cave by the sea where he has happy memories. But there is something else in the cave: a creature, lonely and confused. Together they visit another world where they find wonderful friends, but also deadly enemies.

*"You'll love Brian. Anyone who has struggled with childhood will recognise how he's feeling."*
**TheBookbag.co.uk**

**There Was An Old Fellow From Skye**

A collection of Antony's hilarious limericks for all the family to enjoy.

*"This is a little pot of gold with lots of clever rhymes guaranteed to make you laugh."*

**LoveReading4Kids.co.uk**


**A Tiger Too Many**

Jill is deeply fond of an elderly tiger in London Zoo. But when war breaks out, she makes a shocking discovery. For reasons she can barely begin to understand, the tiger, along with many other dangerous animals in the zoo, is about to be killed. She vows to prevent that from happening, but finds herself virtually powerless in an adults' world. That day, she begins a war of her own, a war to save a tiger.

*"Real edge-of-the-seat-stuff."*

**TheBookbag.co.uk**


You may also enjoy these novels by Antony's father, Paul Wootten:

### The Yendak

*and*

### Whispers on the Wasteland


Find out more about Antony and Paul Wootten, and Eskdale Publishing, at **www.antonywootten.co.uk**.